The Railway Children

E. Nesbit

Adapted by
Mary Sebag-Montefiore

Illustrated by Alan Marks

Reading Consultant: Alison Kelly
Roehampton University

Contents

Chapter 1

Change

It all began at Peter's birthday
party. The servants were just
bringing out the birthday cake,
when the doorbell clanged sharply.

"Bother!" exclaimed Father. "Who can that be? Start without me everyone. I'll be back in a minute."

Peering into the hallway, Peter saw Father leading two men into his study.

"Who are they, Mother?" asked his sister, Phyllis.

"I don't know," said
Mother, frowning.
"Stay here. I'm going
to find out."

Mother disappeared into the
study for ages.

"What's going on?" asked Phyllis.

"We'll just have to wait and see,"
replied Bobbie, the eldest.

Mother emerged just as the front door slammed shut. Bobbie saw a carriage and horses driving rapidly away into the night. Mother's face was icy white and her eyes glittered with tears.

"Where's Father?" demanded Peter, running into the empty study.

"He's gone away." Mother was shaking now. Bobbie reached for her hand and held it tight.

"But he hasn't even packed his clothes," said Phyllis.

"He had to go quickly – on business," Mother replied.

"Was it to do with the Government?" asked Peter. Father worked in a Government office.

"Yes. Don't ask me questions, darlings. I can't tell you anything. Please just go to bed."

Upstairs, the children tried endlessly to work out where Father had gone. The next few days were just as strange.

All the maids left. Then a
FOR SALE sign went up outside
the house. The beautiful furniture
was sold and meals now consisted
of plain, cheap food. Mother was
hardly ever at home.

"What's happening?" asked Peter, finally. "Please tell us."

"We've got to play at being poor for a bit," Mother replied. "We're going to leave London, and live far away in the countryside."

"Father is going to be away for some time," she went on. "But everything will come right in the end, I promise."

Chapter 2
A coal thief

After a long, long journey, they arrived at the new house, late at night. Mother rushed around, digging sheets out of suitcases.

The next day Bobbie, Peter and
Phyllis woke early to explore. They
raced outside until they came to
a red-brick bridge.

Suddenly there was a shriek
and a snort and a train shot out
from under the bridge.

"It's exactly like a dragon," Peter shouted above the noise. "Did you feel the hot air from its breath?"

"Perhaps it's going to London," Phyllis yelled.

"Father might still be there," shrieked Bobbie. "If it's a magic dragon, it'll send our love to Father. Let's wave."

They pulled out their handkerchiefs and waved them in the breeze. Out of a first class carriage window a hand waved back. It was an old gentleman's hand, holding a newspaper.

After that, the children waved every day, rain or shine, at the old gentleman on the 9:15 train to London.

The weather grew colder. Mother sat in her icy bedroom wrapped in shawls, writing stories to earn money for them all.

Bobbie, Peter and Phyllis didn't notice the cold much. They were too busy playing. But one morning, it snowed so much they had to stay inside.

"Please let me light a fire, Mother," begged Bobbie. "We're all freezing."

"Not until tonight, I'm afraid. We can't afford to burn coal all day. Put on more clothes if you're chilly."

Peter was furious. "I'm the man in this family now," he stormed. "And I think we ought to be warm."

Over the next few days Peter began to disappear without saying where he was going.

"I can't understand it," Mother said soon after. "The coal never seems to run out."

"Let's follow Pete," Bobbie whispered to Phyllis. "I'm sure he's up to something."

They trailed him all the way to
the station, and watched him pile
a cart with coal from a huge heap.
Then suddenly, Peter screamed.

A hand had shot out of the darkness and grabbed him by the shoulder.

It was Mr. Perks, the station master. "Don't you know stealing is wrong?" he shouted.

"Wasn't stealing. I was mining for treasure," sulked Peter.

"That treasure belongs to the railway, young man, not you."

"He shouldn't have done it, Mr. Perks," said Bobbie, shocked. "But he was only trying to help Mother. He's really sorry, aren't you, Pete?" She gave him a kick and Peter muttered an apology.

"Accepted," said Perks. "But don't do it again."

"I hate being poor," grumbled Peter, kicking the cobbles on their way home. "And Mother deserves better than this."

Soon after, Mother got very sick. Bobbie didn't know how they were going to pay for her medicines, until she had a brilliant idea.

She wrote a letter to the old gentleman on the 9:15 train to London and asked Mr. Perks to give it to him.

Dear Mr. (we don't know your name),

   Mother is sick and we can't afford the things the doctor says she needs. This is the list:

   Medicine   Port Wine

   Fruit   Soda water

   I don't know who else to ask. Father will pay you back when he comes home, or I will when I grow up.

                              Bobbie

P.S. Please give them to Mr. Perks, the station master, and Pete will fetch them.

The very next day, a huge hamper appeared, filled with medicines, as well as red roses, chocolates and lavender perfume.

A week later, Bobbie, Peter and Phyllis made a banner and waved it at the 9:15 train. It said:

THANK YOU!
SHE IS MUCH BETTER!

But Mother was furious when she found out. "You must never ask strangers for things," she raged.

Bobbie was nearly in tears. "I didn't mean to be naughty."

"I know, my darling," said Mother. "But you mustn't tell everyone we're poor. We have enough to live on — just. Now we won't say any more about it."

Chapter 3

Red for danger

They all felt miserable for upsetting Mother. "I know what will cheer us up!" said Bobbie. "We can ask Mr. Perks for the magazines people leave on trains. They'd be fun to read."

"Let's climb down the cliff and walk along the track to the station," suggested Peter. "We've never gone that way before."

"I don't want to. It doesn't look safe." Phyllis sounded frightened.

"Baby! Scaredy-cat!" teased Peter.

"It's all right, Phil," Bobbie
comforted her. "The cliff isn't
that steep."

"Two against one," crowed Peter.
"Come on, Phil, you'll enjoy it."

Slowly Phyllis followed her
brother and sister, muttering,
"I still don't want to..."

They scrambled down the cliff. Phyllis tumbled down the last bit where the steps had crumbled away, and tore her dress.

Now her red petticoat flapped through the tear as she walked.

"There!" she announced. "I told you this would be horrible, and it is!"

"No, it isn't," disagreed Peter.

"What's that noise?" asked
Bobbie suddenly.

A strange sound, like far off
thunder, began and stopped. Then
it started again, getting louder
and more rumbling.

30

"Look at that tree!" cried Peter. The tree was moving, not like a normal tree when the wind blows, but all in one piece.

All the trees on the bank seemed to be slowly sliding downhill, like a marching army.

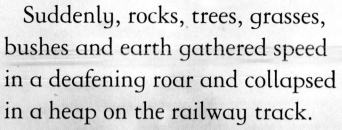

Suddenly, rocks, trees, grasses,
bushes and earth gathered speed
in a deafening roar and collapsed
in a heap on the railway track.

"I don't like it!" shrieked Phyllis.
"It's much too magic for me!"

"It's all coming down," said
Peter in a shaky voice. Then he
cried out, "Oh!"

The others looked at him.

"The 11:29 train! It'll be along any minute. There'll be a terrible accident."

"Can we run to the station and tell them?" Bobbie began.

"No time. We need to warn the driver somehow. What can we do?"

"Our red petticoats!" Bobbie exclaimed. "Red for danger! We'll tear them up and use them as flags."

"We can't rip our clothes!" Phyllis objected. "What will Mother say?"

"She won't mind." Bobbie was undoing her petticoat as she spoke. "Don't you see, Phil, if we don't stop the train in time, people might be killed?"

34

They quickly snapped thin
branches off the nearby trees, tore
up the petticoats and made them
into flags.

"Two each. Wave one in each
hand, and stand on the track so
the train can see us," Peter directed.
"Then jump out of the way."

Phyllis was gasping with fright. "It's dangerous! I don't like it!"

"Think of saving the train," Bobbie implored. "That's what matters most!"

"It's coming," called Peter, though his voice was instantly wiped out in a whirlwind of sound.

As the roaring train thundered nearer and nearer, Bobbie waved her flags furiously. She was sure it was no good, that the train would never see them in time...

"MOVE!" shouted Peter, as the train's steam surrounded them in a cloud of white. But Bobbie couldn't. She had to make it stop.

With a judder and squeal of brakes the train shuddered to a halt and the driver jumped out. "What's going on?"

Peter and Phyllis showed him the landslide. But not Bobbie. She had fainted and lay on the track, white and quiet as a fallen statue, still gripping her petticoat flags.

The driver picked her up and put her in one of the first class carriages. Peter and Phyllis were worried, until finally Bobbie began to cry.

"You kids saved lives today," said the driver. "I expect the Railway Company will give you a reward."

"Just like real heroes and heroines," breathed Phyllis.

Chapter 4
The terrible secret

The Railway Company did want
to reward the children. There was
a ceremony at the station, with a
brass band, bunting and cake.

All the passengers who had been on the train were there, as well as the Railway Director, the train driver, Mr. Perks, and best of all, their own old gentleman.

The Railway Director made a speech praising the children, which they found very embarrassing, and gave them each a gold watch.

When it was all over, the old gentleman shook their hands.

"Oh do come back for tea," said Phyllis.

They climbed up the hill together. Bobbie carried the magazines Mr. Perks had collected for her. He'd made a parcel of them, wrapped in an old sheet of newspaper.

Back home, Mother, Phyllis and Peter chatted with the old gentleman.

Bobbie went into her room, to sort through the magazines. She undid the newspaper wrapping and idly looked at the print. Then she stared.

Her feet went icy cold and her face burned. When she had read it all, she drew a long, uneven breath.

"So now I know," she thought.

It was a report of a spy trial, with a photograph of the accused. It was a photograph of Father. Underneath it said: GUILTY. And then: FIVE YEARS IN JAIL.

Bobbie scrunched up the paper. "Oh Daddy," she whispered. "You never did it."

Time passed. The old gentleman left and it grew dark outside. Supper was ready, but Bobbie couldn't join the others.

Mother came to find her. "What's the matter?" she asked.

Bobbie held out the paper. "Tell me about it," she begged.

Mother told her how Father had been arrested for being a spy. Papers had been found in his desk that proved he had sold his country's secrets to enemies.

"Didn't they know he'd never do such a thing?" Bobbie asked.

"There was a man in his office he never quite trusted," Mother replied. "I think he planted those papers on Father."

"Why didn't you tell the lawyers that?" Bobbie wanted to know.

"Do you think I didn't try everything?" Mother demanded. "We just have to be patient and wait for him to come back to us."

"Why didn't you tell us?"

"Are you going to tell the others now you know?"

"No," said Bobbie.

"Why?"

Bobbie thought hard. "Because... it would only upset them."

"Exactly," said her mother. "But now you've found out, we must help each other to be brave."

They went in to supper together, and though Bobbie's eyes were still red with tears, Peter and Phyllis never guessed why.

Chapter 5

The man in the train

The long, cold winter blossomed into spring, and then summer. Bobbie couldn't bear the way time passed with nothing happening.

Mother was unhappy, Father was in prison, and she couldn't do anything to help. So she wrote a letter. And once more it was to the old gentleman.

Dear Friend,

Mother says we are not to ask for things for ourselves, but this isn't just for me.

You see what it says in this paper.

It isn't true. Father is not a spy.

Could you find out who did it, and then they would let Father out of prison.

Think if it was your Daddy, what would you feel? Please help me.

Love from your good friend,

Bobbie

Soon after she sent the letter,
Bobbie had her twelfth birthday.
Mother gave a bracelet she no
longer wore, Peter and Phyllis made
a cake, and Mr. Perks brought a
bunch of flowers from his garden.

It was very different from her last birthday when she'd had a huge party and lots of presents. This one was happy enough. But Bobbie missed Father so badly, her mind was filled with wanting him.

Then, one late summer's day, when the roses were out and the corn was ripening to gold, Bobbie found it impossible to concentrate on her lessons.

"Please, Mother," she begged. "Can I go outside?"

"Do you have a headache?" asked Mother.

Bobbie thought. "Not really,"
she replied. "I just feel in a daze.
I'd be more alive in the fresh
air, I think."

Mother let her go and Bobbie
found herself walking down to
the station. She felt as if she were
in a dream.

At the station, everyone smiled at her and Mr. Perks shook her hand up and down.

"I saw it in the papers," he grinned. "I'm so pleased. And here comes the 11:54 London train, bang on time."

"Saw what in the papers?" Bobbie asked, puzzled, but Mr. Perks had turned away, blowing his whistle.

As the train drew into the station, Bobbie was astonished to see handkerchiefs fluttering from every window.

Only three people got out. An old woman with a basket of squawking hens, the grocer's wife with some brown-paper packages, and the third...

"Oh! My Daddy, my Daddy!" Bobbie's cry pierced the air.

People looked out of the windows to see a tall thin man and a little girl rush up to each other with open arms.

"I felt something strange was going to happen today," said Bobbie as they walked up the hill, "but I never guessed what."

"Didn't Mother get my letter?" Father asked.

"There weren't any letters this morning," Bobbie replied.

"Mother wrote to tell me you'd found out," he said. "You've been wonderful. The old gentleman has too. He helped them catch the real spy. Now, Bobbie, run ahead and tell Mother and Peter and Phyllis I'm home."

He paused in the garden, looking around at the rich summer countryside with the hungry eyes of someone who has seen too little of flowers and trees and the wide blue sky.

Mother, Bobbie, Peter and Phyllis
stood in the doorway. Father went
down the path to join them.

We won't follow him. In that
happy moment, in that happy
family, no one else is wanted
just now.

E. Nesbit (1858-1924)

Edith Nesbit wrote her
books a hundred years ago,
when most people rode by
horse, not car, and television
hadn't been invented. Her
stories are full of excitement,
adventure and magic.
The original versions are
much longer than Young
Reading books, and they
may seem a little old-fashioned,
but they're well worth reading.
The Railway Children, first published
in 1906, is one of her most famous books.
It has been adapted for the television four
times and has twice been made into a film.

Edited by Susanna Davidson

Series editor: Lesley Sims

Designed by Natacha Goransky

First published in 2007 by Usborne Publishing Ltd.,
Usborne House, 83-85 Saffron Hill, London EC1N 8RT, England.
www.usborne.com Copyright © 2007 Usborne Publishing Ltd.